「Pretend Author」

Jeong Mu

Novella

METRIC

PUBLISHER

Copyright © 2024 by Jeong-mu
All rights reserved.
ISBN: 979-11-986509-5-5

No part of this publication may be reproduced, distributed, or transmitted in any form or by any means, including photocopying, recording, or other electronic or mechanical methods, without the prior written permission of the publisher, except as permitted by U.S. copyright law. For permission requests, contact [zero.proof.all@gmail.com].

First Printing, 2024
METRIC Publisher
3516, 3rd floor, 15-1, Achasan-ro 7-gil
Seongdong-gu, Seoul, 04793

This novel adopts the format of fictional criticism and quotes fictional authors and works in an experimental creation. It is clarified that all the authors and works cited in the text are fictional.

This novel is a work of pure fiction. All characters, events, and places appearing in this work are fictitious. Any resemblance to real events, actual persons, living or dead, or real places is purely coincidental and not intended to represent or depict any actual event or person.

Contents

Email: I'm suffering from serious levels of defamation and threats

10

[1] I've never heard the term "mid-level criticism."

14

Introduction

1. Regarding the controversy over identity in literature 1.1. Limitations and dangers of emphasizing identity / 1.2. The issue of literary figuration and universality
2. The relationship between subject selection and literary authenticity 2.1. Rethinking the concept of authenticity in literary creation / 2.2. The significance and method of representing social minorities
3. Rebuttal to the criticism of following literary trends
    3.1. The dynamism of the literary field in the context of changing times / 3.2. Another possibility of interpreting the paradox inherent in "Pretend Author"

4. The irrelevance of major background and literary creation 4.1. Characteristics of the diversified modern literary ecosystem / 4.2. The harmony of the technical aspects and artistry of literature
5. The ambiguity and danger of the concept of mid-level writers 5.1. Problems with ambiguous and arbitrary classification of writers / 5.2. Need for a literary ecosystem centered on diversity

Conclusion: For a literature of inclusion and solidarity
Appendix: Choi Jeon-young Cultural Critics - "Mid-level Writer" full text

Email: Sending "I've never heard the term 'mid-level criticism'"

56

Email: After reading your article

60

[2] Mid-level Writer

Introduction

1. Trite consciousness and superficial perception of reality in the novel 1.1. Poor literary imagination relying only on sensational subjects / 1.2. The writer's calculating writing behavior that caters to trends
2. Superficial literary authenticity covered with pedantic packaging 2.1. Hollow minority cosplay and the abuse of political correctness / 2.2. The limitations of hollow problem-posing and hypocritical messages
3. The novel reduced to an alibi for the author's excuses
   3.1. The self-contradictory satirical narrative of "Pretend Author" / 3.2. The limitations of hollow problem-posing and hypocritical messages
4. The harmful effects of a science and engineering writer tainted by technological supremacy 4.1. The engineering delusion of quantifying literature / 4.2. Their own league subordinate to the number of clicks and sales
5. The mid-level writer syndrome that has lost creativity and its harmful effects 5.1. The capitalist pathology of novels plastered with imitation and patching / 5.2. The proliferation of a new kind of literary virus that consumes pure literature

Conclusion: The mid-level writer syndrome that condones literature's self-destruction
Appendix: Choi Jeon-young Cultural Critics - "Mid-level Writer" full text

Email: Congratulations, Lee Gim-mi! Grand prize for "Pretend Author"!

111

[3] Letter of Apology -- Kim Bak-chae

115

Author's Words

119

Email:

I'm suffering from serious levels of defamation and threats

Title: I'm suffering from serious levels of defamation and threats
Date: April 9, 2024
Sent : Lee Gim-mi
To : Lawyer Oh Su-jeong

Dear Lawyer Oh Su-jeong,

Hello, this is author Lee Gim-mi. I apologize for contacting you like this. However, I am currently in a situation where I feel trapped and desperately need a helping hand.

The controversy surrounding my debut novel "Pretend Author" has escalated to a serious level. Especially in the past few weeks, there has been a surge in groundless vilification and malicious attacks, causing me immense mental anguish.

Some netizens are fiercely criticizing my novel, claiming that it exploits minority identities, while others disparage it as a low-quality work pandering to commercialism. The problem is that these criticisms are riddled with groundless speculation and gossip.

What's even more concerning is that these criticisms are going beyond the level of constructive criticism of the work, taking on the aspect of personal attacks on my private life and character.

Please make sure to check the attached evidence. (Attached - 10 captured images, 30 comment logs) In particular, I think literary critic Choi Jeon-young, who criticized my work, is behind these attacks. The particularly sharp tone of criticism has increased significantly after his review.

At this rate, not only my creative work but also my daily life and safety will be seriously threatened. I'm looking into ways to legally sanction and hold accountable the perpetrators for intellectual property rights, defamation, insult, etc. What do you think I should do?

I desperately need your wise opinion. As an author, I want to continue my creative activities with pure passion and conviction, but if this situation persists, I may have to give up my literary path. I feel very disheartened and afraid.

Please lend me your wisdom. I want to find a clue to overcome this unfair crisis that has befallen me.

I look forward to your prompt response. I would sincerely appreciate your help.

Sincerely,
Lee Gim-mi.

[1] I've never heard the term "mid-level criticism."

I've never heard the term "mid-level criticism."

Issued: April 1, 2024

- Park Jeong-woo, Cultural Critic

Introduction: The age of diversity and inclusiveness in literature

What is literature? The definition and value of literature have constantly evolved throughout history. Literature, which was the exclusive domain of a small elite class with power in ancient times, gradually began to be popularized with the development of printing technology and the spread of Enlightenment thought. In the 20th century, the emergence of avant-garde movements, modernism, and postmodernism deconstructed and reconstructed the very concept of literature. The attitude that emphasized the inherent purity of literature unfolded in complex aspects within the flow of popular culture, and the boundary between pure literature and popular literature blurred.

Now, after the postmodern era, literature in the 21st century is facing a new phase once again. The development of digital technology and new media has brought changes to the production and consumption of literature, and with the globalization of culture, literature has become a medium that crosses borders and contains diverse voices. With the development of critical theories such as feminism, queer theory, and postcolonialism, the voices of subjects that had been marginalized have risen to the forefront of literature, greatly changing the landscape of literary creation and criticism. Literature is now recognized as an open art genre that aims for universal values, crossing various classes and identities, not as the exclusive property of a few elites.

Given this context, the literary view contained in literary critic Choi Jeon-young's "Mid-level Writer" seems quite anachronistic. The concept of pure literature that he advocates, and the "true author" qualified to create it, reveals an exclusive and hierarchical view of literature that overlooks the diversified terrain of literature now embraced as a dynamic and inclusive cultural field.

In this context, Choi Jeon-young's claim that Lee Gim-mi, a former computer science major, has a tendency towards commercialism based on her educational background, is a biased perception trapped in an overly dichotomous and outdated view of writers. "The very fact that a computer science major who is well-versed in business is writing novels means that 'profitable literature' is the goal, and it's an idea that tries to reduce literature to code and algorithms," he argues. However, this is an overly simplistic and technologically deterministic idea that oversimplifies the complex nature of literary creation.

In fact, looking at modern and contemporary literary history, it has never been the case that only those 'inside' the literary world guaranteed the legitimacy of a writer. Rather, it would not be an exaggeration to say that those who have come into the literary world from outside have expanded the horizons of Korean literature. For example, Yi Kwang-su, a pioneer of modern Korean novels, was from a medical background, while Yi Sang, a painter and film director, was an architecture student. Son Chang-seop and Kim Seung-ok, who were active in the postwar literary world in the

1950s, were both engineering students, with the former majoring in chemical engineering at Yonsei University and the latter in architectural engineering at Seoul National University. Many of those who were actively engaged, such as Han Mal-suk, originally a doctor, and Yi Cheong-jun, a painter, were individuals who entered the path of literature from outside the humanities.

The Korean literary world after the 2000s has also further deepened this pluralistic landscape. With the development of science and technology and changes in the media environment, the majors of writers have become more diverse than ever. Beyond computer science majors, there has been a noticeable increase in writers from natural science backgrounds such as astronomy (Jeong Yi-hyeon), biology (Cheon Un-yeong), and mathematics (Kim Min-jeong). Young writers well-versed in digital media have also begun to make their mark. This suggests that literature is no longer the exclusive domain of graduates from Korean literature or creative writing departments but is transforming into an open and convergent creative activity.

Considering this diversified landscape of writers, the attitude of judging a writer's qualifications and sincerity based on their undergraduate major no longer seems valid. Rather, the diversity of majors is serving as an opportunity to inject new perspectives, ideas, and styles into Korean literature, expanding the horizons of literature. What matters is not the title of the major, but how much literary achievement is accomplished. Choi Jeon-young's view, disparaging and belittling Lee Gim-mi's literary world based solely on her background as a computer science graduate, overlooks the dynamism of this changed literary ecosystem.

1. Regarding the controversy over identity in literature

1.1. imitations and dangers of emphasizing identity

The most noticeable thing in Choi Jeon-young's criticism of novelist Lee Gim-mi is the frame of 'identity.' Choi Jeon-young argues that Lee Gim-mi, as a heterosexual male, is appropriating minority identities that he has not experienced himself, and that this is ethically problematic. In his statement, "Using minorities as material without the experience and concerns of the parties involved undermines the authenticity of literature," we can glimpse an identity-centric attitude that directly links literary authenticity to specific identities.

But the concept of identity that Choi Jeon-young himself advocates is ambiguous. For example, does it mean that in order to create a specific character in a novel, one must have the same gender, race, and class background as that character? According to this logic, it would be impossible to imagine Tolstoy, a male, writing Anna Karenina, or Flaubert, a white man, writing "A Simple Heart," a story of an African black maid. All characters would have to be reduced to the author's own identity, and only autobiographical novels would be considered true literature.

This is an idea that seriously undermines the essence of literary creation. Literature is fundamentally an art based on human 'imagination.' The ability to stand in another's shoes, imagine their life, and empathize is the essence of literature and the core of a writer's qualities. Of course, it goes without saying that this process must be accompanied by thorough self-reflection and literary conscience, but this is not automatically guaranteed by belonging to a specific gender, race, or class. Rather, genuine empathy and insight stem from imaginative efforts to feel the pain of a being different from oneself and to communicate across differences.

In this context, Lee Gim-mi's attempt to portray the voices of others in different circumstances can be evaluated as a literary adventure and a manifestation of a sense of calling. It is at least commendable that he tried to shed light on the lives of sexual minorities and the socially disadvantaged in "Pretend Author." Of course, I acknowledge that Kim Bak-chae's superficial approach in the novel can sometimes be insufficient or problematic. But what's important is not the success or failure of perfect representation, but the 'attempt' itself to gaze at and communicate with the other.

Choi Jeon-young's criticism that "while featuring queer characters, it reinforces prejudices against them" is valid to some extent. However, rather, it is necessary to pay attention to the voice of the narrator in the novel problematizing Kim Bak-chae's perspective. The parts where Kim Bak-chae's superficial representation of minorities is critically reflected upon ultimately show Lee Gim-mi's own self-reflective gaze. In this way, Choi Jeon-young's logic of questioning the author's identity and arguing for a literature that only the parties involved can write overlooks the complex ethics and possibilities that literature possesses.

1.2. The issue of literary figuration and universality

The controversy surrounding identity is ultimately tied to the issue of the universality of literature. How can a particular experience be shaped into a universal human condition? This has been a topic that writers have grappled with since modern literature. This is because revealing universal truths beyond an individual's experience is literature's fundamental desire and role.

Choi Jeon-young points out that Lee Gim-mi "only deals with social issues superficially and does not deeply explore the inner world of the characters." However, this is a rather subjective evaluation. There is no absolute criterion for judging the success or failure of literary figuration. What may seem superficial to one writer may come across as a fresh insight to another reader. What's important is how much power the work wields in generalizing an individual's experience and eliciting empathy, that essential achievement.

In fact, many works evaluated as classics in Korean literary history depict worlds unrelated to the author's direct experience. For example, Han Moo-sook's "Sunani" deals with the lives of families of death row inmates, and Hwang Seok-young's "The Road to Sampo" deals with the emotions of workers in a distorted era of industrialization. Through novels, they gaze at class realities different from their own and convey messages of compassion for alienated beings. It would be difficult to say that their works are superficial or lack authenticity.

The same goes for Lee Gim-mi. From his position, he tried to listen to the voices of minorities and shape a message of empathy for discriminated beings into a novel. This can be seen not as an appropriation or malicious representation of a particular identity, but as an expression of solidarity with the socially disadvantaged and an exploration of universal humanitarianism. The narrative in "Pretend Author" where Kim Bak-chae gains recognition from the literary world through a novel dealing with minority human rights is read as a kind of fable that seeks solidarity of communication and empathy through literature.

Of course, this does not mean that Lee Gim-mi's novel is perfect. The limitations of the way minorities are represented in "Pretend Author" and the ambivalence of the author's attitude need to be critically discussed. For example, Kim Bak-chae's lines such as "Transgender characters should meet a tragic end. They should suffer from discrimination and end their own lives" reveal prejudices and stereotyping that deserve to be pointed out.

However, Choi Jeon-young's attitude of digging into the author's identity and intentions and disparaging literary achievements a priori also has room for reconsideration. While it is important to sharply point out a writer's limitations, the meaning and possibilities inherent in their attempt itself should not be overlooked. What we should pay attention to is the problem consciousness embodied in the work and the questions it poses to us through the narrative. The bold literary experiment that "Pretend Author" conducts by directly addressing sensitive topics in the literary world is sufficiently noteworthy as a provocation that expands the topography of Korean literature, albeit imperfect. Copy.

2. The relationship between subject selection and literary authenticity

2.1. Rethinking the concept of authenticity in literary creation

Along with this controversy over identity, the issue of literary authenticity also emerges as a critical point surrounding novelist Lee Gim-mi. Choi Jeon-young argues that Lee Gim-mi "undermines the authenticity of literature by taking minorities as material without the experience and concerns of the parties involved." But what does authenticity in literature really mean? It is difficult to see it as something limited only to the direct experience of the individual author. In this regard, we need to reconsider the concept of authenticity in literary creation on a more fundamental level.

Literary critic Kim Hyeon sharply dissected the issue of truthfulness in literature through the provocative proposition that "poets must be liars." According to him, a poet must be able to describe even experiences he has not directly had as if they were true, and only through that lie can he reach poetic truth. This acknowledges that literature is ultimately an imaginative act based on the realm of fiction, while at the same time evoking the unique ethics of literature that gazes at humans and the world within that fictional truth.

From this perspective, the authenticity of literature is more related to the author's unwavering spirit of gazing at the world and trying to understand humans, rather than the issue of experiential factuality. The criterion for judging literary authenticity should be how sincerely the artistic conscience and agony toward truth are projected in the work. Therefore, rather than doubting authenticity a priori based on the author's identity or experience, it is necessary to closely evaluate the perception of the world and aesthetic achievement embodied within the work.

Of course, in shaping the life of the other, it goes without saying that thorough field research, coverage, and deep communication with the parties involved must precede. However, this is not automatically guaranteed by having a specific identity, but rather requires constant self-reflection, other-oriented thinking, and a devoted artistic spirit. In this context, Lee Gim-mi's "Pretend Author" can be seen as embodying its own authenticity and ethics in that it sought to listen to the voices of marginalized minorities in Korean society and explore a literary imagination of solidarity and empathy.

2.2. The significance and method of representing social minorities

Choi Jeon-young's perception that problematizes literature dealing with minority issues itself also seems to have room for reconsideration. For him, the issue of minority representation is dismissed as the epitome of commercialism that excessively caters to trends. However, considering the way literature has transformed in close relationship with various social agendas since the postmodern era, this is an overly simplified evaluation.

In fact, looking back at literary history, representing the voices of social marginalized people and raising issues of discrimination and oppression has been one of the important roles of literature. Social problem novels of the Victorian era in 19th-century England, African American literature in the United States, postcolonial literature in the Third World, etc. have established themselves as literary trends that expose social contradictions and represent voices of resistance from the standpoint of the alienated. They have acted as a driving force for social transformation by exercising literature's unique imagination to deconstruct the dominant order from a marginal perspective and seek alternatives.

In this tradition, Lee Gim-mi's focus on minority issues such as LGBTQ, disability, and feminism can be evaluated as a manifestation of a socially engaged literary spirit and an ethical practice. Of course, in this process, it is necessary to be wary of minority representation remaining at a superficial level. While putting the voices of the marginalized at the forefront, one should not fall into the error of hasty generalization or stereotyping. A writerly insight is required that delves into the concrete lives and concerns of individual minorities while seeking to explore universal human conditions beyond their particularities. This will be an arduous process that requires fierce gaze and reflection, not turning away from otherness and unfamiliarity.

In that sense, the part where the protagonist Kim Bak-chae writes a novel with queer material to fit the code of the literary world can be read as a meta-satirical take on minority representation. It is a part that sharply points out the reality where minority narratives are appropriated as a kind of cultural capital and consumed within the literary field. This is not so much a problem of minority representation itself but makes us reflect on the attitude of strategizing and commodifying it in a literary way. In short, Lee Gim-mi's problem consciousness seems to go beyond the mere level of subject matter and question the complex dynamics surrounding the representation of minorities within the

Korean literary world and the conditions of authenticity itself.

3. Rebuttal to the criticism of following literary trends
3.1. The dynamism of the literary field in the context of changing times

Along with the issue of literary authenticity and ethics, the mixed reactions of the literary world to Lee Gim-mi's work reflect the complex dynamics within the Korean literary field. Choi Jeon-young argues that Lee Gim-mi is strategically dealing with minority issues following the trend of the literary world. He claims that "the contradiction is revealed that the author himself is following the literary trend that he satirized in 'Fake Author'." However, this seems to stem from a rather essentialist view of literature that presupposes the literary field as a fixed and unchanging entity. In fact, looking back at the history of modern Korean literature, literature has always been in the flow of change, listening to the demands of the times.

In the early 1900s, during the enlightenment period, literature took on a purposeful character in the face of the historical proposition of national enlightenment and the promotion of independence consciousness. In the 1920s and 1930s, during the dark period of Japanese colonial rule, the emergence of proletarian literature and sharp debates surrounding the sociality and popularity of literature unfolded. In the post-war period, the political nature of literature was explored amid the scars of war and ideological confrontation. Since the industrialization period, issues of the subject of literature, such as national literature, labor literature, and women's literature, have been actively explored. In this way, literature has been a dynamic entity that has breathed with the times and newly sought its social value.

The growing interest in minority literature such as feminism and queer literature in today's literary world also needs to be understood in the context of the interaction between literature and society. Since the 2010s, minority issues have emerged as major agendas both inside and outside the literary world, intertwined with the resurgence of feminism, controversy, the Me Too movement, and the disability rights movement throughout Korean society. These changes can be interpreted as a reflection of social reality and consciousness, and as a new ethical demand that literature must bear. In fact, as revealed in Lee Gim-mi's "Pretend Author," the movement to literarily portray new agendas in Korean society such as minority rights and gender inequality is in itself a sufficiently meaningful writerly attitude to be evaluated. The problem is whether it remains at a superficial level or leads to a true moment of recognition.

Of course, there is also a risk of commercialistic tendencies intervening in this process. For some writers, minority representation may be misused as a means of self-display or acquisition of cultural capital rather than universal empathy. However, this is a matter of specific evaluation of individual works and authors and cannot be dismissed as a problem of all minority narratives in general. Rather, the literary world's movement to embrace diverse voices into the primal field of literature itself should be understood as a natural flow reflecting the changing times.

3.2. Another possibility of interpreting the paradox inherent in "Pretend Author"

On the other hand, Choi Jeon-young points out the contradiction that while Lee Gim-mi criticizes the trend of the literary world through "Pretend Author," he himself is pandering to it. However, there is no need to interpret the literary world satire in "Pretend Author" only as simple satire or denunciation. Rather, that paradoxical situation setting itself may be part of the author's intended aesthetic strategy.

Choi Jeon-young criticizes Lee Gim-mi's writerly consciousness as also remaining at a superficial level. The gist is that "while satirizing the literary world in the novel, he himself panders to commercialism." But isn't this also a superficial reading that overlooks the complexity of the text, caught up in Choi Jeon-young's own dichotomous thinking?

In fact, "Pretend Author" has ample room to be read as an accumulation of serious concerns about literature. In the work, Kim Bak-chae agonizes, saying, "I want to write pure literature, but reality is not easy." He also confesses, "As a writer, I want to resist the absurdities of the world, but compromises are also necessary to make a living." This can be said to be an expression of fundamental agony surrounding the raison d'être of literature and the identity of the writer.

Of course, there is room for self-justification in this part as well. However, it is impossible to overlook the fact that while portraying the self-portrait of a writer immersed in commercialism, he tried to gaze at the existential pain behind it. Kim Bak-chae's agony of conflict between literary authenticity and reality compromise ultimately evokes the tension between literature and capitalism itself.

In this way, within the structure of self-reflective metafiction, the thematic consciousness of "Pretend Author" that delves into the writer's spirit and literary view is a point that Choi Jeon-young's linear criticism is missing. We need to take a more multi-faceted view of the courageous writerly exploration that attempts to textualize the dialectical struggle itself between literature and capital, authenticity and compromise.

"Pretend Author" has a significant character as a 'metafiction.' This is because it satirically depicts the complex status that minority narratives occupy within the Korean literary field since the 2000s. The mechanism by which minority becomes a literary resource and circulates as cultural capital, the process by which existing canonical power is paradoxically solidified due to this, etc. form major motifs throughout "Pretend Author."

Therefore, the literary landscape in "Pretend Author" functions not merely as a mimetic reflection of external reality, but as a space for problematization and reflection in itself. Through this, Lee Gim-mi is shaping the mechanism of literary field power that appropriates and commodifies minority, and the tension and dynamics between literary authenticity and commercialism. The narrative development in which Kim Bak-chae strategically utilizes queer narratives can be said to paradoxically reflect the zeitgeist conditions the author is in. It is in this sense that "Pretend Author" is a meta-allegory that concisely shows the self-portrait of the Korean literary world.

In that sense, the position of the author himself, the target of satire within the satire of the literary world, can also be read as an opportunity for self-reflective awareness, not just an object of criticism. Lee Gim-mi reminds us that he himself is also a writer subject with a foot in the problematic reality and raises fundamental questions about literary authenticity and the perception of reality. This can be seen as a manifestation of a kind of meta-consciousness that self-reflectively gazes at the ethics and paradox inherent in the act of novel writing itself.

The "contradiction" pointed out by Choi Jeon-young can rather be a testament to Lee Gim-mi's unique self-reflective consciousness about his own position as a writer and the act of writing.

In fact, the narrative strategy of "Pretend Author" evokes the fundamental paradox that literature faces, that is, the dilemma surrounding the "ethics of representation." The point that literature is an act of reflecting and representing reality, but that act of representation inevitably has no choice but to reduce the complexity of reality and cut it from a specific perspective. This can be said to be a fundamental limitation and ethical dilemma inherent in all literary acts. And this contradiction is also a paradox brought about by the ethical project of literature that seeks to represent the voices of others and expose reality.

The moment the life of a minority is represented, that narrative is inevitably exposed to the risk of objectification and stereotyping. Even an ethical attitude that tries to listen to marginal voices may, despite good intentions, essentialize a particular identity or appropriate it as a literary commodity. This paradox is also a difficult problem faced by all writers who have pondered the ethics of representation. Perhaps Lee Gim-mi is shaping this very point, the dilemma of the impossibility of representation, through "Pretend Author."

Therefore, we ask, along with the question of what "true minority literature" is, about the ethics and impossibility of the act of minority representation itself. And this leads to a question about the very conditions of existence of literature. Can literature fully reflect reality? Is it possible for literature to ethically engage with the other and reality? How can literature's ethical project and aesthetic figuration coexist? These questions can be seen as an extension of the problem consciousness raised by "Pretend Author."

4. The irrelevance of major background and literary creation

4.1. Characteristics of the diversified modern literary ecosystem

In addition to the discourse landscape within the literary world, the question surrounding the identity of the creative subject also emerges as an important issue in the evaluation of Lee Gim-mi's literature. Choi Jeon-young points out Lee Gim-mi's commercial tendencies based on the fact that she is a writer from a computer science background. He argues that "the very fact that a computer science major well-versed in business is writing a novel is for the purpose of 'profitable literature,' and it is an idea that tries to reduce literature to code and algorithms." However, this is a perception that is caught up in an overly dichotomous and outdated view of writers.

In fact, looking at modern and contemporary literary history, it has never been the case that only those from 'inside' literature guaranteed the legitimacy of a writer.

Rather, it would not be an exaggeration to say that those who have flowed in from various academic backgrounds and occupations have expanded the horizons of Korean literature. For example, Yi Kwang-su, a pioneer of modern Korean novels, was from a medical background, while Yi Sang, a painter and film director, was an architecture student. Son Chang-seop and Kim Seung-ok, who were active in the postwar literary world in the 1950s, were both engineering students, with the former majoring in chemical engineering at Yonsei University and the latter in architectural engineering at Seoul National University. Many of those who were actively engaged, such as Han Mal-suk, originally a doctor, and Yi Cheong-jun, a painter, were individuals who entered the path of literature from outside the humanities.

The Korean literary world after the 2000s has also further deepened this pluralistic landscape. With the development of science and technology and changes in the media environment, the majors of writers have become more diverse than ever. Beyond computer science majors, there has been a noticeable increase in writers from natural science backgrounds such as astronomy (Jeong Yi-hyeon), biology (Cheon Un-yeong), and mathematics (Kim Min-jeong). Young writers well-versed in digital media have also begun to make their mark. This suggests that literature is no longer the exclusive domain of graduates from Korean literature or creative writing departments but is transforming into an open and convergent creative activity.

Considering this diversified landscape of writers, the attitude of judging a writer's qualifications and sincerity based on their undergraduate major no longer seems valid. Rather, the diversity of majors is serving as an opportunity to inject new perspectives, ideas, and styles into Korean literature, expanding the horizons of literature. What matters is not the title of the major, but how much literary achievement is accomplished. Choi Jeon-young's view, disparaging and belittling Lee Gim-mi's literary world based solely on her background as a computer science graduate, overlooks the dynamism of this changed literary ecosystem.

4.2. The harmony of the technical aspects and artistry of literature

On the other hand, Choi Jeon-young is concerned that the mindset of a computer science major will "reduce literature to code and algorithms." However, this is nothing more than a technologically deterministic idea that simplifies the complex attributes of literary creation. In fact, literature is inherently the product of a precise construction act mediated through language. Writers build their fictional worlds based on their own principles, orders, and systems of selecting and arranging words and sentences. In that sense, the act of literature itself belongs to the realm of techne.

Of course, literature as techne cannot be reduced to the dimension of mechanical and regular code. The ambiguity, fullness, and openness of literary language harbor depths that cannot be captured by any fixed algorithm. However, that does not mean that literature remains in a mysterious realm unrelated to technology. Rather, literature has always sought new formal leaps through the dialectical interaction of techne and poiesis.

In fact, many innovative moments in literary history are closely related to the development of science and technology. The invention of the printing press enabled the mass production and distribution of books, leading to the rise of the modern novel. The development of camera and film technology had a profound impact on the aesthetics of realism and modernism, and computers and the Internet triggered new narrative experiments such as hypertext literature. In this way, literature has expanded the horizons of genre, form, and style by closely interacting with the technology of the times.

In this context, Choi Jeon-young's assertion that Lee Gim-mi's science and engineering background will undermine her literary merit seems hasty. Rather, the meticulous composition and logical thinking of an engineering student may contribute to enhancing the coherence of the work. In fact, "Pretend Author" showcases its own meticulous aesthetic of composition through meta-fictional layers, complex plot structures, and unique character settings. Of course, the essence of literature lies in aesthetic achievement. Skill or sophistication of plot does not guarantee being moved. However, the dichotomy that an engineer's thinking is incompatible with artistry also seems to have room for reconsideration.

In short, it is necessary to acknowledge the dimension of techne inherent in literature and directly face the fact that technological progress can open new literary imaginations. We need to listen to the literary worlds of science and engineering writers represented by Lee Gim-mi without prejudice and approach with an open attitude the possibility that they may present different literary milestones from before. This is also an act of breaking away from stereotypes about the traditional image of writers and moving toward a more flexible and expansive concept of literature.**The ambiguity and danger of the concept of mid-level writers**

4.3. Problems with ambiguous and arbitrary classification of writers

The controversy surrounding Lee Gim-mi's undergraduate major is ultimately in contact with the long-standing conflict surrounding the criteria for 'pure' and 'popular', and literary legitimacy within the Korean literary world. Choi Jeon-young refers to Lee Gim-mi as a 'mid-level writer' and expresses concern about the "gap between technical writing and literature" and the "negative impact on the Korean literary world." However, there are several problems inherent in this logic. Above all, the concept of 'mid-level writer' itself is ambiguous and arbitrary. It is closer to a convenient rhetoric based on Choi Jeon-young's personal taste and view of literature.

The hierarchical division that categorizes writers' competence and achievements into beginner, intermediate, advanced, etc. is nothing more than a subjective evaluation that is difficult to verify. The method of classifying writers into A, B, C classes according to the aesthetic standards of an individual critic and judging them a priori is, in a different light, a typical case of the language of empowered criticism. It is closely related to the ideological attitude of normalizing particular literary values and solidifying power relations within the literary world.

Moreover, the intermediate and advanced classification that understands writers in the model of skilled artisans in the apprenticeship method is fundamentally anachronistic. The hierarchical class division borrowed from the artisan model of traditional society is far from the modern and contemporary view of art, characterized by the concept of the artist as an independent creator. Since the 20th century, the understanding of artists has shifted from a romantic notion centered on 'talent' and 'inspiration' to placing emphasis on the unique concerns and worldviews of individual artists.

In this context, the very naming of 'mid-level writer' reflects a biased perspective that does not recognize the individuality and uniqueness of the writer. It is an outburst of an ahistorical and hierarchical view of literature that lines up writers and distinguishes superiority and inferiority, which conflicts with the concept of literature since the modern era. Moreover, if such subjective and arbitrary criteria become entrenched as the exclusive standard of the literary world, it should not be overlooked that it can be misused as a tool to strengthen the vested interests of the established literary world.

4.4. Need for a literary ecosystem centered on diversity

In addition, Choi Jeon-young cautions against the "negative impact on the Korean literary world" of 'mid-level writers' represented by Lee Gim-mi. However, this is a perception arising from a monistic view of literature that understands literature as a singular trend and tendency. In fact, Korean literature has always been a dynamic field where writers with various individuality and styles compete and clash. This was also a process in which different literary ideals and practices collided and expanded the horizons of literary history.

In particular, the Korean literary world after the 2000s has shown several characteristic changes. Amid the socio-cultural shifts such as the solidification of the IMF and neoliberal system, the development of digital culture, and the emergence of new sensibilities, new literary trends and senses erupted. Representative examples include the spread of private novels and labor novels delving into capitalist daily life, the revival of the SF/fantasy genre, and the literary awakening of the non-regular youth generation.

Of course, concerns and vigilance about these new trends have also existed. Warning voices have been raised, mainly from the critics' circle, about the weakening of literariness and commercialistic tendencies. The landscape of novel mass production centered on large publishing companies, the rampant genre literature focusing on reader interest, and the collusion with mass media are certainly points that should be the subject of reflection and criticism. However, it should be avoided that this vigilance negates the pluralistic literary terrain itself or preemptively disparages new literary attempts.

It is necessary to keep in mind that diversity and plurality are the factors that make a literary ecosystem healthy. Korean literature has dynamically evolved through competition and tension between heterogeneous voices crossing the mainstream and the non-mainstream, the pure and the popular. Therefore, an attitude of leaving open the possibilities of new literary trends and humbly listening is necessary. This is also a critical ethic to protect the inherent diversity and vitality of literature.

From this perspective, the emergence of new groups of writers represented by Lee Gim-mi can be a nutrient to expand the horizons of Korean literature. We need to pay attention to the possibility that their works will challenge existing literary norms and canons and present heterogeneous sensibilities, and furthermore, relativize mainstream literature and serve as an opportunity to reflect on the view of literature itself. The coexistence of diversity and difference is what guarantees the dynamism of literature, and when we accept this fact, we can open a more inclusive and open field of literary discourse.

Of course, in this process, the role of criticism also needs to be redefined. Rather than normalizing a particular style and faction and establishing exclusive criteria, the task of mediating different literary projects and individualities to form meaningful tensions. The task of objectively evaluating the aesthetics of each voice and spectrum and opening a place for communication so that more voices can play their part. That will be the virtue required of critics and the ethics of criticism in the age of diversity.

In this sense, the limits of Choi Jeon-young's criticism are clear. An exclusive view of literature, dichotomous schemas, and a sense of hierarchy within literature are factors that hinder the diversity and vitality of literature. Recognizing the unique value of individual literatures, not one literature, and acknowledging the coexistence of multiple literatures, not universal literature. This should be the basic premise that criticism should embrace and the starting point for opening a new era of literature. Choi Jeon-young needs to directly face this pluralistic and dynamic landscape of Korean literature. This is also an act of breaking down the boundaries of literature and expanding its possibilities.

So far, we have examined various issues surrounding novelist Lee Gim-mi. Questions raised at various levels, such as the ethics of representation and sincerity in literature, the problem of literary authenticity and thematic consciousness, the issue of the characteristics of the discourse landscape within the literary world and aesthetic standards, and the perception of the author's undergraduate major and technology, ultimately lead to a fundamental question. What is literature and what role should it play?

What mode of existence should literature take in a changing society? To answer this question, a more macro and fundamental contemplation seems necessary.

Conclusion: For a literature of inclusion and solidarity

So far, we have critically read Choi Jeon-young's critique "Mid-level Writer" and illuminated the consciousness of the problem and aesthetics embodied in Lee Gim-mi's novel "Pretend Author." In this process, we argued for the need to deconstruct essentialist notions and exclusive norms about literature and seek a more pluralistic and dynamic concept of literature. Recognizing that literature is not a self-sufficient entity with a fixed essence and identity, but a historical construct that breathes with the times and changes. Reflecting on the hierarchy and power inherent in literature by questioning the identity of the literary subject. And accepting the process itself of expanding the horizons of literature with various individuality and styles coexisting as the driving force of literary history. In line with these questions and explorations, we can revisit the mode of existence of literature and the meaning of literary acts on a more fundamental level.

The fact that literature is fundamentally an exploration of human existence and a way of looking at the world anew. The fact that the act of literature itself is a process of crossing boundaries and exercising an imagination of empathy and solidarity with others. When we focus on these inherent attributes of literature, we re-recognize the values of inclusion and solidarity required of literature today. This is because only literature that listens to unfamiliar voices and gazes at the reality outside the boundaries can provide the imaginative resources to overcome this era of division and hatred.

In that sense, the literary attempt shown in Lee Gim-mi's "Pretend Author" has great implications. The writer's consciousness of deconstructing the existing exclusive literary norms and ethically responding to marginalized voices. An open attitude to think of literature not as an institution subordinate to power and capital, but as a free play of the spirit and an opportunity for reflection on life. These all question the raison d'être and possibilities of literature on a more fundamental level. Contrary to Choi Jeon-young's view of literature that "true literature should not pander to commercialism and popularity, but pursue the inherent value of art," Lee Gim-mi problematizes the relationship between artistic acts and capitalist reality itself.

That is why we need to pay attention to Lee Gim-mi's literary experiment. This is because it can be an opportunity to reflect on the sociality of literature and the meaning of intervention, going beyond the myth of exclusive and self-contained pure literature. Literature that seeks to move from the ivory tower to the square, from individual imagination to communal solidarity. It is a declaration of a literary person who will not participate in the reality of silence and alienation, and a practice of imagination that looks at the world anew and seeks the possibility of change.

Of course, we are not unconditionally advocating for Lee Gim-mi. It goes without saying that a rigorous evaluation of the achievement and limitations of literary figuration must follow. The important thing is an open attitude that does not lean toward a particular style or faction but acknowledges and listens to differences and individuality as they are. Only then can we delicately read the socio-cultural foundation and context that enable a writer's voice. We can critically lead the writer to deeper realism and fierce aesthetic exploration. Thus, we can guide literature to serve as a medium that sheds new light on the world and expands our sensibilities.

The fact that literature can never be a resting place for finite beings. The fact that literature is an open path that endlessly asks us questions and requests adventures. Only on the basis of this humble recognition of literature can we move towards a better future of literature. Acknowledging one's own finitude and limitations, but never losing the thread of solidarity and imagination toward others within it. That would be the task and calling given to all of us who engage in literature. In that sense, we need to pay attention to the new literary trends represented by Lee Gim-mi and "Pretend Author," and actively participate in the literary world's overall exploration toward the diversity and inclusiveness of literature. Only an open attitude that breaks down the boundaries of literature and embraces more voices can open the way for the literature of our time.

Today, what we urgently need is not literature as 'absolute truth' but literature as 'endless exploration.' Literature not as a fixed essence or dogma, but as a dynamic entity that constantly evolves with different voices and senses competing. Literature as a creative act that crosses boundaries and divisions and opens up a wider horizon of empathy and solidarity. Recognizing and respecting the values of inclusion and diversity, we need to explore the possibilities of this new literary imagination. We need to build a pluralistic and dynamic literary ecosystem. Only then can we expect that literature will become an imaginative source that presents hope and vision for another world, beyond an era rife with hatred, discrimination, and inequality.

Email

Sending "I've never heard the term 'mid-level criticism'"

Title: Sending "I've never heard the term 'mid-level criticism'"
Date: March 26, 2024
Sent: Park Jeong-woo Cultural Critics
To: Author Lee Gim-mi

Dear Author Lee Gim-mi,

Hello, this is Park Jeong-woo.

I recently came across critic Choi Jeon-young's article "Mid-level Writer" and was greatly shocked. I could not hide my astonishment at the speculative assertions filled with prejudice and misunderstanding, and the malicious criticism that insults your sincerity as a writer.

I believe your novel "Pretend Author" satirized the unreasonable aspects of the literary world and showed the pure spirit of a writer who does not want to pander to commercialism. In terms of minority representation, the humanistic concern to give voice to the socially weak stood out.

In response to Choi Jeon-young's superficial criticism, I tried writing an article titled "I've never heard the term 'mid-level criticism'." I sought to fundamentally revisit the essence of literary acts and the issue of the writer's sincerity, and to illuminate the sharp questions your novel poses to our time.

While writing, I realized. That literature is ultimately a noble emanation of the spirit that seeks to understand humans and the world, and a product of intellect imbued with the conscience and conviction of the writer. I think you are someone who has upheld that literary spirit without yielding even in the face of absurdity in the literary world.

I hope this letter provides some small comfort to you who must be hurt and struggling right now. I always support and stand by you as you silently walk the path of creation. And I want to be a source of strength by your side, especially during difficult times.

I really wanted to tell you. That I look at you with pride and respect as an artist and as a friend. I will approach the task of listening to your anguish and agony with the utmost gratitude.

Please take good care of your health. I look forward to seeing you again with good works, and I send you my unwavering friendship and trust.

Sincerely,

Park Jeong-woo.

Email

After reading your article

Title: After reading your article
Date: March 20, 2024
Sent: Author Lee Gim-mi
To: Choi Jeong-young

Choi Jeon-young, I read your critique "Mid-level Writer" well.

Frankly, I believed that you of all people would deeply understand my work and support it wholeheartedly, so I feel devastated and utterly disappointed to see this article full of sarcasm.

To dismiss my desperate concern to listen to minorities and reveal their existence as mere commercial ambition and an accompaniment to winning a literary award. It's shocking and saddening.

I have gained great strength from your encouragement and support. I thought our relationship of sharing literary views and worldviews and our artistic concerns was special. But after reading your article that judges my novel only in terms of commercialism and political correctness, I felt a deep sense of betrayal.

Where has the artistic spirit we have so painstakingly honed and the pure faith in literature gone? The figure you reveal in that article is nothing more than an opportunistic and biased critic. Our friendship and support for art were merely superficial, it seems.

It's very sad and miserable. The concerns and conversations we shared, the future of literature we dreamed of together, seem to be crumbling. But nevertheless, I will not stop this writing. I will uphold my conviction as a writer even in front of people who consider it vulgar.

The path I must walk as a writer is rough, but I intend to silently devote myself while keeping my place. Someday, I hope you too will recognize my literary spirit, and by then, I hope we will be friends who truly understand each other.

I wish your health and good luck in your future.

Lee Gim-mi.

[2] Mid-level Writer

Mid-level Writer

- Choi Jeong-young Cultural Critics

Introduction: The emergence of 'Mid-level Writers' that have thrown the literary world into confusion

A new wave is surging in the Korean literary world. It is the rise of 'Mid-level Writers' who are immersed in commercialism and pander to the tastes of the public. As Kim Bak-chae, the protagonist of Lee Gim-mi's novel "Pretend Author," declares, "I will become famous with a poor work that panders to commercialism and popularity," they betray the spirit of pure literature and captivate readers with sensational subjects and provocative strategies. The literary landscape depicted in "Pretend Author" starkly reveals the bare face of our literary world. It is nothing short of a signal flare alerting us that the fall of literary values and the writer's spirit has reached a serious level.

In this grim situation, novelist Lee Gim-mi's work "Pretend Author" is drawing attention. However, this is not positive attention, but attention as a prime example that reveals the bare face of 'mid-level literature.' This work, as a self-portrait that blatantly shows the behavior of a novice writer tamed by commercialism, concentratedly reveals the crisis facing Korean literature today.

The novel ostensibly satirizes the behavior of the literary world through the debut process of Kim Bak-chae, a novice writer, but behind it is a projection of the author herself. Kim Bak-chae employs all sorts of schemes to gain fame and wealth through novels. He attracts readers' attention with sensational topics, consumes minority codes by following trends, and even induces the attention of critics with a meta-writing that seems to admit to being a problematic writer. In that sense, this work is closer to a self-justification wearing the guise of metafiction.

Lee Gim-mi's actions shown in this novel are the epitome of the 'Mid-level Writer' syndrome. While problematizing commercial writing that panders to tastes and popularity, she herself is not free from such behavior. Rather, she mass-produces works that fit the code of the literary world and critics, mindful of their eyes. This contradictory move is projected through the character Kim Bak-chae, but fails to lead to self-reflection on the part of the author herself.

Such a 'Mid-level Writer' syndrome is not limited to Lee Gim-mi as an individual. The contraction of the print market and the spread of digital media, and the resulting reorganization of the readership, act as new variables for writers today. Rather than embodying the writer's spirit within the framework of pure literature, there is a spreading trend of abusing keywords and forms that can quickly attract readers' attention. It is a strategy of preempting specific subjects and enticing readers with media-friendly writing, a rampant behavior of indulging in provocative narratives that trigger a kind of conditioned reflex.

Of course, experimentation with new literary styles and sensibilities befitting the changing times is necessary. It is self-evident that literature should break away from stale conventions and more actively engage with real-world issues and seek alternatives. However, what is found in 'mid-level writers' seems far from genuine concerns or literary anguish. Rather, what stands out in them is commercial expediency and careerist agility.

If Lee Gim-mi's novel shows the epitome of such a 'mid-level writer,' then we also have the responsibility to critically examine and be wary of this. Dissecting their actions and exposing what structural ills the current literary climate carries, this is also the calling of a critic who must uphold the spirit of pure literature and cultivate a healthy literary ecosystem.

Thus, this article intends to analyze the various aspects of the 'mid-level writer' syndrome revealed in Lee Gim-mi's "Pretend Author" from multiple angles, and through this, directly face the bare face of Korean literature in crisis. Mobilizing the sharp scalpel of criticism to cut out the ills of commercialism and restore the inherent raison d'être and values of literature, that should be the critic's response to the times.

1. **Trite consciousness and superficial perception of reality in the novel**

1.1. Poor literary imagination relying only on sensational subjects

While reading "Pretend Author," one cannot help but stick out one's tongue at the trite problem consciousness and superficial perception of reality in the novel. Kim Bakchae's inner thoughts, such as "If I write about LGBTQ+ as a novel subject, I'll win a literary award. Should I also aim for buzz by sparking feminist controversy?" blatantly show the author's vulgar problem consciousness. This work clings to shallow writing as if interesting arrangement of subjects and provocative narrative development alone can captivate readers. The strategy of putting forth problematic subjects such as the tragic end of a transgender character and the issue of discrimination against sexual minorities to stimulate readers' voyeurism is so reminiscent of the provocative content overflowing in the online media era.

The novel indiscriminately appropriates issues from LGBTQ+ to feminism, disability rights, and more, in a reckless manner. However, these subjects are not literarily shaped or connected to thematic consciousness within the work. They merely remain as a strategic arrangement to captivate readers' eyes with provocative spectacles. It even gives the impression of simply listing real-time search keywords on a portal site.

What's even more problematic is that such selection of subjects reflects the author's superficial perception of reality. Lee Gim-mi does not deeply explore the hardships or struggles of the lives of the socially disadvantaged. She is only engrossed in exposing their pain and sensationally consuming it. The behavior of dealing with social issues on the surface without a sincere approach is proof that she regards all these subjects as literary tools and is far from a genuine perception of reality.

The narrative of "Pretend Author" is unbelievably shoddy. It is close to a listing of scenes patched together for the sake of interest. The main events and conflicts in the novel are treated superficially, failing to create tension, and the causal relationships are also extremely clumsy. Eventually, the author even shows an attitude of satirizing her own narrative, which seems to expect a secret collusion with the reader but only causes distrust in the narrative.

Above all, the characters are depicted very flatly. They are close to signs representing specific types. The protagonist Kim Bak-chae is depicted only as an archetype of an opportunist thirsty for social success, without showing inner conflicts or psychological depth. The surrounding characters, such as senior writers and critics, also do not escape fragmentary images and trite dialogues. This is proof of the author's poor character creation ability.

The narrative of "Pretend Author" is unbelievably shoddy. It is close to a listing of scenes patched together for the sake of interest. The main events and conflicts in the novel are treated superficially, failing to create tension, and the causal relationships are also extremely clumsy. Eventually, the author even shows an attitude of satirizing her own narrative, which seems to expect a secret collusion with the reader but only causes distrust in the narrative.

Above all, the characters are depicted very flatly. They are close to signs representing specific types. The protagonist Kim Bak-chae is depicted only as an archetype of an opportunist thirsty for social success, without showing inner conflicts or psychological depth. The surrounding characters, such as senior writers and critics, also do not escape fragmentary images and trite dialogues. This is proof of the author's poor character creation ability.

In short, Lee Gim-mi's novel writing revealed in 'Fake Author' is nothing more than a practice that deceives readers by relying on sensationalism and conventionality. The absence of authorial consciousness or artistic imagination renders this novel mere shallow entertainment. What unfolds in her writing is nothing but a cynical worldview and commercialism. This is a forgetting of the essence of literature and an act of pandering to public taste, in a word, a loss of literary imagination.

1.2. The writer's calculating writing behavior that caters to trends

An even more serious problem is that her novel does not simply end as a single piece of poor work. "Pretend Author" blatantly reflects the author's own opportunistic writing behavior. In short, this work is a projection of a calculative authorial figure immersed in commercialism. In that sense, Kim Bak-chae's actions in the novel can be said to be a self-portrait of Lee Gim-mi herself.

In the novel, Kim Bak-chae constantly follows the flow of the literary world. For him, creation is close to a kind of trend game that keeps up with the latest fads. His behavior of selecting the themes of his works while checking what gets attention and what subjects can attract readers' interest is as meticulous as conducting market research. He even attempts a meta-interpretation of himself to justify his commercial writing.

However, paradoxically, this aspect of Kim Bak-chae makes one intently gaze at Lee Gim-mi as a writer. This is because her own creative method is none other than writing that rides the current, making profitable literature. Lee Gim-mi meticulously combs through the style of surrounding writers and the trends of the literary world, and calculates what subject matter and style to put forth as a game changer.

She constructs the framework of her work in a highly strategic and imitative way.

This is the typical behavior of mid-level writers. Rather than building their own literary world, they are engrossed in following proven recipes and quickly adapting to trending grammar. They are only good at the skill of selecting and assembling 'sellable' elements, rather than the depth of the subject or the quality of the work. Within the shrewdness of following trends, the fundamental question of literature disappears, and only marketability remains as the criterion for judgment.

Unfortunately, Lee Gim-mi's debut work "Pretend Author" is a compendium of such strategies. Selection of sensational and provocative subject matter, imitation of techniques that attract readers' attention, and even an attitude that ironically gazes at the author herself. All of these are nothing more than strategic choices to conform to today's commercial trends surrounding literature. Above all, such behavior reveals the limitation of satirizing one's own writing in the novel but failing to lead to self-reflection and introspection. Although she pretends to satirize herself by borrowing the form of metafiction, this is also nothing more than a calculated pose to seduce readers.

As a result, "Pretend Author" seems difficult to have meaning beyond provocative self-advertisement. It is a novel that blatantly projects the nerves of a writer accustomed to self-aggrandizing writing in the era of social media. However, this is far from the essence of literature. Writing that is engrossed only in marketability to the point of losing the literary world that reflects and communicates genuinely with readers, is in the first place questionable whether it deserves to be called literature.

2. Superficial literary authenticity covered with pedantic packaging

2.1. Hollow minority cosplay and the abuse of political correctness

Another unpleasantness that Lee Gim-mi's "Pretend Author" gives to readers stems from its hypocritical attitude. Although she pretends to listen to the voices of social minorities, she only degrades their identities into tools of the novel. It's close to pedantic pretensions and ostentatious hypocrisy devoid of inner authenticity, taking the attitude of so-called 'political correctness.'

Let's look at a scene from "Pretend Author." The protagonist Kim Bak-chae borrows the voices of minorities for the sake of winning a literary award. There is a part where he expediently selects a subject, saying, "Queer material is trending these days. If I write about that as a story theme, I might be able to aim for a literary award." He then does not hesitate to reveal his calculation to create a female character who discusses feminism to draw attention.

On the surface, his actions may seem like the aspect of a progressive writer who listens to marginalized voices. However, this is nothing more than a facade. For Kim Bak-chae, minority characters are only tools to gain the attention of readers, and he does not genuinely try to understand their inner selves. His inner monologue, "I have to write what readers like. Depth isn't really important," plainly shows this.

This is nothing short of violence that objectifies the existence of minorities and even consumes their pain as a novel. Rather than fully conveying the voices of the parties involved, he adapts them to his own taste. In the novel, Kim Bak-chae even refers to the queer character he depicts as a "marketing cool girl who puts her sexuality forward." This passage blatantly reveals his perception that commodifies minority identities and treats them as secondary beings.

This attitude is reminiscent of Lee Gim-mi herself. While dealing with minorities in her novel, she also remains at a superficial representation. Although she presents queer characters, she fails to delicately portray their inner landscapes or unique sensibilities. Even in the part where Kim Bak-chae writes a novel with queer content, he merely "arranges a few provocative and sensational scenes." While presenting a feminist character, it is difficult to find sharp insights into gender issues.

This is the result of borrowing trending discourses in a cursory manner without genuine concern for minority issues. Behind the pretentious attitude of trying to appear as a progressive writer, there is no agony or sense of solidarity as someone directly involved. She is only engrossed in cosplaying as a victim to attract the attention of readers and receive favorable reviews from critics.

In particular, the scene where Kim Bak-chae claims, "Using minority issues was consideration for readers," symbolically shows the hypocritical attitude of the writer. It's as if he's pretending to be devoted to social justice through literature while glorifying himself as a writer who empathizes with the pain of the weak and represents their voices. This is closer to using the suffering of others as a shield to claim his own innocence.

In short, Lee Gim-mi's novel exploits minorities but never stands in solidarity with them. This hypocritical attitude, filled with superficial interest in the weak and pedantic self-aggrandizement, is far from true literary practice. The loss of the writer's spirit leads to the loss of the novel's inner truthfulness. She is only engrossed in commercializing and spectacularizing literature, wearing the guise of political correctness.

2.2. The limitations of hollow problem-posing and hypocritical messages

Unfortunately, the problem consciousness of "Pretend Author" remains at the level of declarative messages. Although it ostensibly takes a socially critical attitude, it is actually difficult to find sharp critical consciousness or subversive imagination. The fundamental limitation of this work is that it is full of superficial problem-posing about reality but fails to lead to literary reflection.

In the novel, Kim Bak-chae says, "Equality and human rights are just packaging for writers." While seeming to reinforce the work's provocative message, this is also a passage that reveals the author's true feelings. While throwing out heavy topics such as minority rights, sexual commodification, and gender inequality, genuine problem consciousness is missing.

On the surface, the work covers all kinds of social issues. However, this is nothing more than listing provocative subjects and trending agendas. When looking into it, only superficial descriptions and trite messages remain. It merely relies on clichés such as "the transgender protagonist eventually meets a tragic end" or "the young generation is a victim of an unequal structure." It is difficult to find a deep awareness of what the problem is and what changes are needed.

Moreover, as can be seen in "Pretend Author," Lee Gim-mi fails to connect social agendas to the inner landscapes of characters. This is plainly shown in the passage where Kim Bak-chae says, "Should I create a female character who discusses feminism? Gender issues are hot these days." Although he presents a female character who discusses feminism, there is no description that actually delves into gender issues. Kim Bak-chae and the characters around him seem to embody certain social values and ideologies, but specific perceptions of reality or emotional lines are absent. As revealed in Kim Bak-chae's line, "A transgender character should meet a tragic end, it's a cliché of queer stories," they are merely reduced to signs representing specific types.

This also reflects Lee Gim-mi's own concerns. For her, characters are nothing more than stereotypes colored with social issue keywords. She only focuses on superficial issues without showing their inner concerns and wounds in a complex way. There is criticism of society in the foreground of the story, but in fact, the hollowness of character portrayal is more prominent.

"I want to be a writer who listens to the voices of the hurt and alienated." Kim Bak-chae's confession at the end of the novel represents the voice of the author Lee Gim-mi. However, this is self-deception and a pretentious declaration on the part of the author. Her social criticism in the work is full of superficial problem-posing and declarative attitudes, lacking genuine solidarity or insight.

Such a hollow problem-posing and superficial message delivery method rather proves the author's ignorance and irresponsibility. The complex gaze and sharp insight, which are the virtues of the novel, are nowhere to be found. Only hypocritical and self-righteous messages filled with self-righteousness under the pretext of social righteousness remain.

This results in fading the social critical function of literature itself. When keen problem consciousness about social reality is organically embodied within the aesthetics of the novel, literature can finally exert the power of imagination that newly illuminates the world. However,

"Pretend Author" lacks such a vivid perception of reality and the ability to give shape to it.

In the end, the social criticism Lee Gim-mi shows is nothing more than an empty pose. The limitation of throwing out important topics but failing to show profound literary reflection. The echo of her voice shouting for social justice is nothing but a hollow echo. Her behavior of relying on favorable slogans without genuine problem consciousness is the hypocrisy and self-deception of literature.

In particular, the scene of a deal with the editor of a large publishing company that appears in the novel is meaningful. The editor reveals a strategy to market Kim Bak-chae by actively utilizing the image of a 'problematic writer.' And Kim Bak-chae readily agrees, saying, "If it can attract the attention of readers, that's the reason for a writer's existence." It is a passage that blatantly shows the aspect of compromising in front of commercial interests while glorifying oneself as a writer who exposes the absurdities of the literary world.

These actions ultimately attest to Lee Gim-mi's own calculative behavior. While packaging himself as a pioneer who creates trends, in reality, he is only riding the current. While boldly claiming to open up new horizons in literature, in the end, obsession with success and careerism dominates his inner self. From the appearance of flattering the mainstream literary world while shrewdly finding gaps to break into, the essence of the so-called 'mid-level writer' is blatantly revealed. The attitude of an ambitious junior who flatters the older generation while simultaneously threatening the positions of seniors. This is the typical behavior of mid-level writers of this era.

As a result, his actions show the aspect of a careerist who tries to settle within the power structure of the existing literary field, rather than innovating the power structure of the existing literary field itself. Contrary to the packaged words, behind it lies the desire for power and the obsession with material success. The miserable act of turning a blind eye to one's own trickster actions while pretending to be the standard-bearer of 'new literature.' In a landscape where literary authenticity has disappeared and only shabby ambitions prevail, it is none other than this.

3. The novel reduced to an alibi for the author's excuses

3.1. The self-contradictory satirical narrative of "Pretend Author"

Along with the issue of literary authenticity and ethics, the mixed reactions of the literary world to Lee Gim-mi's work reflect the complex dynamics within the Korean literary field. Choi Jeon-young argues that Lee Gim-mi is strategically dealing with minority issues following the trend of the literary world. He claims that "the contradiction is revealed that the author himself is following the literary trend that he satirized in 'Fake Author'." However, this seems to stem from a rather essentialist view of literature that presupposes the literary field as a fixed and unchanging entity. In fact, looking back at the history of modern Korean literature, literature has always been in the flow of change, listening to the demands of the times.

In the early 1900s, during the enlightenment period, literature took on a purposeful character in the face of the historical proposition of national enlightenment and the promotion of independence consciousness. In the 1920s and 1930s, during the dark period of Japanese colonial rule, the emergence of proletarian literature and sharp debates surrounding the sociality and popularity of literature unfolded. In the post-war period, the political nature of literature was explored amid the scars of war and ideological confrontation. Since the industrialization period, issues of the subject of literature, such as national literature, labor literature, and women's literature, have been actively explored. In this way, literature has been a dynamic entity that has breathed with the times and newly sought its social value.

The growing interest in minority literature such as feminism and queer literature in today's literary world also needs to be understood in the context of the interaction between literature and society. Since the 2010s, minority issues have emerged as major agendas both inside and outside the literary world, intertwined with the resurgence of feminism, controversy, the Me Too movement, and the disability rights movement throughout Korean society. These changes can be interpreted as a reflection of social reality and consciousness, and as a new ethical demand that literature must bear. In fact, as revealed in Lee Gim-mi's "Pretend Author," the movement to literarily portray new agendas in Korean society such as minority rights and gender inequality is in itself a sufficiently meaningful writerly attitude to be evaluated. The problem is whether it remains at a superficial level or leads to a true moment of recognition.

Of course, there is also a risk of commercialistic tendencies intervening in this process. For some writers, minority representation may be misused as a means of self-display or acquisition of cultural capital rather than universal empathy. However, this is a matter of specific evaluation of individual works and authors, and cannot be dismissed as a problem of all minority narratives in general. Rather, the literary world's movement to embrace diverse voices into the primal field of literature itself should be understood as a natural flow reflecting the changing times.

3.2. Another possibility of interpreting the paradox inherent in "Pretend Author"

In fact, the narrative strategy of "Pretend Author" evokes the fundamental paradox that literature faces, that is, the dilemma surrounding the "ethics of representation." The point that literature is an act of reflecting and representing reality, but that act of representation inevitably has no choice but to reduce the complexity of reality and cut it from a specific perspective. This can be said to be a fundamental limitation and ethical dilemma inherent in all literary acts. And this contradiction is also a paradox brought about by the ethical project of literature that seeks to represent the voices of others and expose reality.

The moment the life of a minority is represented, that narrative is inevitably exposed to the risk of objectification and stereotyping. Even an ethical attitude that tries to listen to marginal voices may, despite good intentions, essentialize a particular identity or appropriate it as a literary commodity. This paradox is also a difficult problem faced by all writers who have pondered the ethics of representation. Perhaps Lee Gim-mi is shaping this very point, the dilemma of the impossibility of representation, through "Pretend Author."

Therefore, we ask, along with the question of what "true minority literature" is, about the ethics and impossibility of the act of minority representation itself. And this leads to a question about the very conditions of existence of literature. Can literature fully reflect reality? Is it possible for literature to ethically engage with the other and reality? How can literature's ethical project and aesthetic figuration coexist? These questions can be seen as an extension of the problem consciousness raised by "Pretend Author."

4. The harmful effects of a science and engineering writer tainted by technological supremacy

4.1. The engineering delusion of quantifying literature

At the root of Lee Gim-mi's mid-level writer behavior lies his unique background. His background as a science and engineering writer who majored in computer science acts as a code that runs through his writing. And this sometimes leads to a literary view obsessed with technological supremacy, manifesting in a deformed form within the work.

Lee Gim-mi's engineering mindset revealed here and there in "Pretend Author" is astonishingly dangerous. Kim Bak-chae declares, "I can create a database of the components of a novel and create a bestseller equation. It's about developing an algorithm that predicts readers' reactions." It's an idea as if even the process of literary creation can be replaced by a kind of optimization algorithm. The moment one tries to judge literature by quantitative standards, the possibility of deep insight into the human inner world and aesthetic figuration is blocked. Kim Bak-chae's way of thinking also reflects the limitations of the author Lee Gim-mi. For him, a novel is nothing more than an object that can be quantified and modeled as much as possible according to data laws. This engineering thinking is also involved when setting the personalities and actions of characters. "Find the types of characters that readers will enthusiastically like through data analysis. Based on that, design the characters," reveals the danger of reducing literature to a process of producing standardized products in Kim Bak-chae's thoughts.

This is a desecration and disparagement of literature. It is an idea that directly denies the fact that literature is the manifestation of free imagination, not calculable laws. It is an anti-literary and anti-human act that drives literature into the isolationism of data supremacy and erases the complexity and individuality of the human inner world.

"I can create a database of the components of novels and create a model that predicts readers' reactions." After receiving a literary award, Kim Bak-chae reveals this ambition. It is a dangerous delusion for a writer, stemming from the idea of technically reducing literature. It is an attempt to confine literature to the realm of data and calculability, forgetting the fact that it is an artistic act based on human innate creativity and imagination.

This is likely to lead to the danger of negating the inherent value and dignity of human beings. The moment one tries to judge literature by quantitative standards, the possibility of deep insight into humanity and delicate aesthetic figuration is fundamentally blocked. There is a risk that literature will be reduced to a product that is uniformly 'produced' according to a formula for commercial success.

The problem is that this perception is projected throughout the creative process, damaging the literariness. Lee Gim-mi's engineering mindset reveals harmful effects in every single way of weaving the plot and setting the characters' actions. While treating the novel as if it were a standardized mass-produced product, deep insights into human beings are lost.

This is a desecration and disparagement of literature. It is an idea that directly denies the fact that literature is a verbal art that penetrates the complexity of the human inner world and the contradictions of reality, and therefore is a manifestation of free imagination that cannot be standardized. Furthermore, this is an act that may encourage anti-literary and anti-human trends that lead to the erasure of humanity and standardization.

Of course, the changes in the new media environment and the demands of the readership in the digital age cannot be ignored. Literature can also attempt to incorporate cutting-edge technology in the creation and distribution process. However, all of that should be nothing more than a tool to expand human-inherent thinking and emotion, not an end in itself. Technology is meaningful only when it serves to embody the inherent value of human beings.

In that sense, Lee Gim-mi's engineering writing is a dangerous idea. This is because it not only degrades literature into a tool of shallow quantification but also fundamentally damages the aesthetic realm unique to novels. His delusion of reducing literature to the level of mere 'technique' cannot be accepted. It is a dangerous idea that falls into data supremacy, turning away from the absolute value of human dignity.

4.2. Their own league subordinate to the number of clicks and sales

This is a desecration and disparagement of literature. It is an idea that directly denies the fact that literature is a verbal art that penetrates the complexity of the human inner world and the contradictions of reality, and therefore is a manifestation of free imagination that cannot be standardized. Furthermore, this is an act that may encourage anti-literary and anti-human trends that lead to the erasure of humanity and standardization.

Of course, the changes in the new media environment and the demands of the readership in the digital age cannot be ignored. Literature can also attempt to incorporate cutting-edge technology in the creation and distribution process. However, all of that should be nothing more than a tool to expand human-inherent thinking and emotion, not an end in itself. Technology is meaningful only when it serves to embody the inherent value of human beings.

In that sense, Lee Gim-mi's engineering writing is a dangerous idea. This is because it not only degrades literature into a tool of shallow quantification but also fundamentally damages the aesthetic realm unique to novels. His delusion of reducing literature to the level of mere 'technique' cannot be accepted. It is a dangerous idea that falls into data supremacy, turning away from the absolute value of human dignity.

4.3. Their own league subordinate to the number of clicks and sales

An even bigger problem is that this technological supremacist thinking is spreading within the literary world. Recently, as a group of 'data-based writers' has rapidly increased, there are even signs of the formation of a so-called 'their own league.' They are shaking up the literary ecosystem with the number of clicks and sales as absolute criteria. At the forefront of this stands none other than Lee Gim-mi.

In the novel, through the mouth of Kim Bak-chae, Lee Gim-mi spouts. "I write based on the number of clicks, sales, and readers' interests. That's the way for a writer to survive and the future of literature." Although it is packaged as a declaration of 'new literature' on the surface, when looking into its inner workings, it is nothing more than writing tainted by shallow successism. The sloppy creative behavior of indiscriminately pulling and attaching elements that help with popularity is brazenly carried out.

What is particularly problematic is the fact that this perception is spreading among novice writers as if it were natural. In the novel, Kim Bak-chae does not spare the following advice to young aspiring writers. "Write what readers want. You have to adjust the quality of the writing and select topics accordingly." It is as if the essence of creation lies in targeting the interests of readers, and literature is also an object that must be 'customized' according to demand like a product.

This is nothing more than pandering to commercialism, forgetting the essence of literature. It is a landscape where the subjectivity of creation has disappeared and marketability and popularity reign supreme as gold and jade. All of this is brazenly carried out under the favorable pretext of so-called 'data-based creation,' so how deplorable is this?

An even greater evil is that this fundamentally distorts the relationship between writers and readers. The writer is no longer an artist who moves the hearts of readers with delicate emotions and thoughts, but is degraded into a technician who manufactures products following the tastes of the public. On the contrary, the reader is objectified into a passive being that consumes shallow pleasures, not an active subject who discovers the truth of life while resonating with works. This is a situation where the function of communication and reflection that literature should have is fundamentally paralyzed.

As the current situation is like this, a gloomy shadow is cast over the Korean literary world. Young writers who want to walk the path of literature based on pure passion and humanism are losing their place, and only those who cling to giant platforms and data power in pursuit of immediate results are dominating the field. The current trend, tainted by the golden calf mentality and forgetting the unique raison d'être of literature, raises a sense of crisis.

Of course, it is necessary to seek new literary styles and distribution methods suitable for the changing media environment. It is self-evident that literature also needs to actively utilize the innovative results brought about by technological advances. However, it would be problematic if this leads to racing towards cheap populism for the sake of clicks and sales, ignoring the essence of literature. If one only pursues commercial results, literature will eventually lose its reason for existence.

In this context, the actions of 'mid-level writers' represented by Lee Gim-mi are more than worrying symptoms. They are only engrossed in short-sighted expediency, not realizing that their writing is undermining the dignity and vitality of literature. It is self-evident that the boomerang that such behavior will bring will return to themselves. This is because writing that fails to move the hearts of readers with genuine communication and reflection is bound to self-destruct.

5. The mid-level writer syndrome that has lost creativity and its harmful effects

5.1. The capitalist pathology of novels plastered with imitation and patching

For those referred to as 'mid-level writers,' the loss of creativity is an inevitable evil. Rather than building a creative world based on pure passion and unique literary ideals, they are engrossed in imitating the works of senior writers and patching together trending codes. Literally, it is a landscape where only the products of imitation and assembly are mass-produced, with originality and artistic spirit missing.

Lee Gim-mi's "Pretend Author" also starkly shows the bare face of such 'mid-level literature.' Throughout the novel, scenes reminiscent of senior writers' works blatantly appear. The part depicting college creative writing club activities gives the impression of directly borrowing clichés from existing campus novels, and the hardships of the debut process are limited to following the formula of established literary world satire novels. In the end, all of these narratives fail to escape the repertoire of trite and conventional storytelling.

The problem is that the behavior of imitation and patching is spreading throughout the literary world. Writers immersed in the so-called 'bestseller formula' have lost creative thinking and individual style, and are engrossed in copying the composition and style of popular works. The recent landscape of the Korean literary world is that similar derivative works pour out like a flood whenever a successful work appears.

In this climate where imitation and plagiarism are rampant, the uniqueness and artistic sincerity of individual writers lose their place. For writers immersed in market logic and chasing the formula of bestsellers, literature is ultimately nothing more than a means of producing content with high marketability. For them, a novel is not a product of complete creation, but is no different from a disposable product that is easily assembled and consumed like a convenience store lunch box. Literary conscience has long disappeared, and the mid-level writer syndrome obsessed with 'sellable' writing is a symptom that shows the dark side of the Korean literary world.

Within a structure where large publishing companies and huge capital dominate the production and distribution of literature, novice writers become engrossed in conforming to the bestseller formula rather than creative adventures. The landscape of so-called 'hit works,' with large-scale marketing and film and drama adaptation contracts flying in immediately after publication, compressively shows the structural ills of such a literary world. A group of writers obsessed with commercial success rather than pure artistic passion, and publishing capital preoccupied with sales performance rather than the discovery of quality works. All of these factors are intertwined, promoting the loss of creativity and literary sincerity.

As a result, the artistic perfection and aesthetic achievement of novels are pushed to the back burner, and media exposure and sales volumes have become the yardsticks for evaluating works. In the distorted landscape of the publishing industry where only quantitative expansion prevails over quality books, it is distant to expect genuine literary achievements and the writer's spirit. The behavior of the group referred to as 'mid-level writers' is an inevitable byproduct of such structural pathology of the literary ecosystem.

5.2. The proliferation of a new kind of literary virus that consumes pure literature

The evil effects of the mid-level writer syndrome do not end there. In "Pretend Author," Kim Bak-chae says, "It's important to be armed with trendy subjects and provocative stories. Perfection? That's a secondary issue." This passage not only shows how superficial the writing of mid-level writers is but also suggests that the overall dignity and vitality of Korean literature are facing a serious crisis.

The writing of these people, who only appeal to technique and wit without delving into the inherent truth of life and human beings, is like a new type of virus that undermines the unique raison d'être of literature. As revealed in Kim Bak-chae's line, "What readers want is shock and stimulation. Just arrange the political codes that suit the tastes of literary award judges well," for them, a novel is nothing more than a product of calculated senses, not complete creation.

As a result, literary acts based on a pure artistic spirit are losing their place, and only ambition for commercial success has become the driving force for creation. Kim Bak-chae's remark, "Things like artistry aren't important at all," blatantly shows the mindset of the mid-level writer group. Because of them, the literary spirit that seeks to sublimate life into art while breathing with the times is being threatened. A landscape unfolds before our eyes where Korean literature is subordinated to capital and the tastes of the public, losing even its reason for existence.

On the other hand, at the end of Lee Gim-mi's novel "Pretend Author," there is an apology posted by the protagonist Kim Bak-chae on his SNS. Through this apology, the fictional character Kim Bak-chae conveys an explanation for the satire of the literary world, reflection on the issue of minority representation, and an apology for the tendency toward commercialism. However, this is, after all, just a scene in the novel, and it is difficult to see it as the voice of the author Lee Gim-mi herself.

Rather, this apology further highlights the issue of the author's sincerity. It even gives the impression that she is trying to evade responsibility by putting forth a fictional character. Rather than the author's own reflection and introspection being genuinely revealed, it leaves an aftertaste as if it functions as a shield to avoid criticism. This in turn reflects the aspect of the 'mid-level writer' raised in the novel.

Such insincere apologies and excuses show another evil of the 'mid-level writer' syndrome. Self-reflection and repentance have disappeared, and only the rhetoric of evasion of responsibility and deception are rampant. This is a aspect that symbolically shows the landscape of the literary world of this era, which has lost its original stance for literature while pandering to capital and the demands of the public.

This trend ultimately leads to the collapse of the public's trust in literature. The novels of mid-level writers, plastered with monotonous stories, stereotypical characters, and sensational subjects, instill in readers the misunderstanding and disillusionment that "literature is ultimately like this." Their works, which do nothing more than provide light amusement, are raising questions about the inherent value that literature should possess.

In particular, the absence of criticism and literary communication is further encouraging this trend. The formation of an uncritical discourse field that gives generous praise to commercially successful works and shows cold indifference to serious works that do not receive attention. The disappearance of meticulous criticism that delves into the depths of the text, and the prevalence of superficial reviews that are limited to subjective impressions or superficial introductions of works and authors. All of these factors are giving a free pass to the mid-level writer syndrome.

As a result, literature is facing a crisis of losing its raison d'être in the Korean literary world today. Works that are nothing more than shallow amusement in the guise of literature dominate the market, and in a landscape where uncritical acceptance of them prevails, the sprouts of pure literature have become difficult to take root. Popular culture replaces the authority and place that literature has lost, and readers intoxicated with cheap pleasure are turning their backs on literature.

Of course, the responsibility for this crisis cannot be attributed solely to mid-level writers. Rather, it is necessary to directly face and reflect on the structure itself that produces and condones them. Publishing capital immersed in commercialism, losing the essence of literature, the loss of the critical spirit that delves into the depths of works, and the passive attitude of readers intoxicated with cheap fun, etc. Awakening and reflecting on the essence of the crisis that shakes the entire Korean literary ecosystem, this should be the starting point for confronting the 'mid-level writer' syndrome.

Conclusion: The mid-level writer syndrome that condones literature's self-destruction

So far, we have critically examined Lee Gim-mi's "Pretend Author" through the lens of the 'mid-level writer' syndrome. His behavior of objectifying novel creation with eyes only for commercial success starkly shows the aspect of the crisis that is shaking the Korean literary world. This is a problematization that does not end with merely pointing out the limitations of a single author. It is also an act of evoking the serious ontological crisis that literature faces today.

In the behavior of 'mid-level writers' represented by Lee Gim-mi, we witness the bare face of capitalist realism riddled with falsehood and deception. The act of reducing literature to marketability and entertainment, and trading the life of literature to the logic of capital. This is nothing short of suicidal behavior that fundamentally undermines literature's own reason for existence and essence. And it is the essence of the mid-level writer syndrome to contribute to this suicidal behavior.

In that sense, Lee Gim-mi's "Pretend Author" is closer to a self-confession than a satirical novel. Although he pretends to satirize himself, he ends up revealing the limitations of the writing he embodies. This is because the behavior of a mid-level writer without self-awareness and the creative method tamed by commercialism are fully projected into the novel. The author fails to realize that the blade of satire is directed at himself.

What we need now is a movement of self-reflection and innovation throughout the literary world against such a mid-level writer syndrome. It is urgent to raise the writer's spirit that revisits the essence of literary creation and restores lost literary conscience. In addition, meticulous criticism that delves into the depths of works, and the active participation of readers who try to seriously communicate with literature are also required. Only when the entire literary ecosystem establishes a critical spirit and reflective dialogue that goes beyond the logic of capital can a clue be found to break through the current crisis.

Above all, it is important to create a foundation to protect and nurture those who want to walk the path of literature with a pure spirit. Creating a literary environment where young and talented writers can maintain their dignity as artists without being swept away by the current of commercialism. That would be the starting point for going beyond the mid-level writer syndrome and a prerequisite for a new era of literature.

Korean literature is now standing in front of a fundamental question asking for its reason for existence.

The mid-level writer syndrome is a signal flare alerting us of such a crisis and, paradoxically, a cautionary example suggesting the direction literature should take. The landscape of Lee Gim-mi's "Pretend Author" and the discourse surrounding it poses a valuable problem consciousness to us. A question that anyone who wants to walk the path of literature must face at least once. It would be to prove that literature is not a commodity subordinate to capital, but a noble reflection of the human spirit, the artist's struggle and practice toward truth and freedom.

Email:
Congratulations, Lee Gim-mi! Grand prize for "Pretend Author"!

Title: Congratulations, Lee Gim-mi! Grand prize for "Pretend Author"!
Date: February 29, 2024
Sent : Choi Jeon-young
To : Lee Gim-mi

Lee Gim-mi,

I heard the news that you won the grand prize at the OO Literary Awards for "Pretend Author." Congratulations! You should celebrate yourself, you amazing writer!

Winning the grand prize right away in your first literary award challenge with a full-length novel, I'm so happy and grateful. I know you've had a hard time silently continuing your work. The unwavering literary spirit of not compromising with commercialism, the warm gaze of listening to the voices of minorities and the socially weak. It was a world where it was hard to survive as a writer.

But you went your own way silently. Writing that pursues truth without compromise, the conscience of an artist who does not remain silent in the face of injustice. Your works have always embodied that noble spirit. I was proud of you and respected you.

This award is a moment when your writer's spirit shines. Sincere writing eventually becomes known to the world and resonates. Although it must have been a rough journey, don't you feel like that hardship is now being rewarded with great glory?

I also want to talk in detail about the themes and quality of "Pretend Author" soon. I have many questions about your literary world and concerns as a writer. What literature is and what values it should aim for, what questions we should ask through novels. I want to discuss all night like before and have a heart-fluttering conversation.

Recently, my daily life has been busy, so I haven't been able to contact you often, which I deeply regret. Taking this joyous occasion, I must meet you and have a drink to relieve the pent-up feelings. You were already a wonderful writer, but now the world has recognized your shining talent.

Take good care of your health, and I look forward to even better works in the future. I send you my unwavering support and support! See you soon.

Your friend who will always be a supportive presence by your side,
Choi Jeon-young

[3] Letter of Apology

Letter of Apology

Hello, this is Kim Bak-chae.

I am writing this to express my stance and apologize for the controversy and criticism surrounding my debut novel "Pretend Author."

First, I sincerely apologize for making you uncomfortable regarding the satire of the literary world in my work. It is true that there were some sharp descriptions in the process of fictionally depicting reality, but it was by no means intended to slander any specific person or group. Nevertheless, I apologize for causing discomfort to senior writers and readers who have been paying attention.

In addition, I am deeply reflecting on the issue of minority representation. I acknowledge that rather than truly listening to and empathizing with the voices of the socially disadvantaged, I remained at a superficial level of description and consumed their lives as material for the novel without deep reflection. In the future, I will strive to write with a more delicate and responsible attitude to empathize with and stand in solidarity with the pain of others.

I am acutely aware that the controversies surrounding my work and actions have led to criticism of damaging the spirit of pure literature and leaning towards commercialism. As a writer, I also have a responsibility to uphold the nobility of creative acts and the purity of writing, but I am ashamed that I forgot my duty in my obsession with reader attention and the buzz around my work. From now on, I will walk the path of a writer who pursues the essence of literature.

I think I have caused great disappointment to readers by showing a side of myself that is still too lacking compared to the love and interest I have received. I would like to take this opportunity to express my gratitude to those who have consistently supported my work and to those who have not hesitated to give me sharp rebukes and advice. I will humbly engrave your voices and make every effort to repay you with better works.

Once again, I deeply apologize for my shortcomings. I will return to my original intentions and silently walk the path of a writer with only love and pride for literature. I ask for your unwavering interest and affection. Thank you.

Kim Bak-chae

"Pretend Author"
<The End>

[Author's Words]

What qualifies one to be a writer?

What qualifies one to ponder the qualifications of a writer?

May 2024

Jeong Mu

www.ingramcontent.com/pod-product-compliance
Lightning Source LLC
LaVergne TN
LVHW041710060526
838201LV00043B/659